THE THURSDAY CREATURE

William Heinemann Ltd
Michelin House, 81 Fulham Road,
London SW3 6RB

LONDON   MELBOURNE   AUCKLAND

First published 1990
Text © 1990 Sam McBratney
Illustrations © 1990 Terry McKenna
ISBN 0 434 93089 X
Produced by Mandarin Offset
Printed in Hong Kong

A school pack of SUPERCHAMPS 7–12
is available from
Heinemann Educational Books
ISBN 0 435 00091 8

THE THURSDAY CREATURE

SAM MCBRATNEY

Illustrated by
TERRY MCKENNA

HEINEMANN · LONDON

Chapter 1

FEAR IS CATCHING, did you know that? The first time I saw the Thursday Creature, it taught me that. Fear can spread through a crowd like fire through a forest of trees.

Thursday is our school's Youth Club night. Mr Ford takes it and also Mrs White who teaches infants. We hold quizzes and play board games and snooker and things. Last month we had five-a-side football and I still have the bruises where Stephen Bishop hacked me. I called him a hacker to his face.

'You're a hacker, Bishop,' I said.

He said he only went for the ball – and shortly after that Mrs White sent us both off for arguing. She's a lovely teacher who allows little children to swing on her, but what a referee! I don't think she's ever kicked a football in her whole life.

That night – the night of the Thursday Creature – we had the quarter-finals and the semis of the Quoits Competition. Now I have to admit that until that night I had no idea that the game of quoits existed,

the quoit.

and my friend Melanie thought they had something to do with polo and Prince Charles. It's even a quirky word – not quite 'quote' and not quite 'quiet' but something in between. Still, it might come in handy when you're playing Scrabble.

Anyway, a quoit is a rubber ring the size of a plate. You throw it over a cord and hope your opponent drops it, in which case you win a point. The first to get ten points wins the game.

If I'd been knocked out in the first round I would have thought this the most boring game ever invented – except that I won. And I kept on winning on account of my superb skill and wonderful athleticism. Mum says it was my ballet classes that did it; she thinks ballet gives you a bendy body.

I beat Corinna Bell in the first round,

Jim Fender in the second round and by the semis I was very keen on Quoits and ready to turn professional when I left school. Craig Harvey bit the dirt next, and Melanie was so excited for me.

'Guess who you're playing in the final, Jenny!'

'Stephen Bishop,' I said.

'He's awfully good.'

But does he do ballet, I thought.

Mr Ford looked at the clock and said that we had to clear up our rubbish as we were running out of time. The final would have to wait until next week. This didn't suit me at all. I was keyed-up, my confidence sky-high after so many glorious victories – and now I would have seven long nights to lie in bed wondering if Bishop would hammer me ten-nil.

As Melanie and I swept crushed potato crisps off the Hall floor with long, graceful sweeps of our brushes, we happened to spot Corinna Bell up on the stage doing nothing at all.

'Lazy loafer,' muttered Melanie. She's not fond of Corinna Bell, and she's not the only one, because Corinna says too much about people and she says it too loudly.

'I bet you couldn't guess what she wants to be when she grows up,' said Melanie.

'A woman?'

'A civil engineer. She cuts bridges out of magazines. Nobody else I know loves bridges like that.'

'So what, Melanie?' I said. 'They're just as interesting as stamps.'

'Or rocks, I suppose. My brother's room is full of stupid rocks.'

People, we decided, could be funny. Melanie and I were putting away our brushes when we heard a commotion starting up in the corridor that leads to the Hall. Naturally we went to have a look, because we like excitement as much as anybody else.

Well, we found a throng of people there. Somewhere in the middle were three small kids who told us how a dragon was loose in the school. And

they weren't whispering, either. They were spreading the electrifying news as loudly as they knew how.

They'd seen it near the boys' toilets. It was such a horrible big slobbering beast that merely to tell of its sheer awfulness made one of the little boys bawl his eyes out, and I for one knew that he must have seen a dragon, all right.

Seven-year-olds don't act that good.

Chapter 2

'Don't be such a silly boy!' shrieked Mrs White, who was all of a twitter as the panic began to spread. 'There are no such things as dragons, children, they do not *exist*. Dry those eyes at once. And wipe that nose!'

As Mrs White pounced with a clean hanky, about twenty people set off up the gloomy corridor in a mass huddle, and I was one of them. Dragons are high on my list of things that make Life interesting. It was like one of those old black and white horror movies when the whole town turns out to finish off poor old Frankenstein's monster.

'Aaaa! It's there. I saw it!'

The shriek came from the front of the crowd – which came to a halt, I can safely say, as if we were soldiers on parade. I saw it too, but not very clearly. A vivid flash of light lit up the blunt end of the creature's incredible head. Its mouth gaped open horribly, and there were teeth in that mouth. Then it let loose a sound like no noise ever heard before and the bones in my legs turned to pure jelly. Something grabbed my arm with the power of a monster crab and I nearly died – but it was only Melanie holding on for dear life.

'It's really real! Oh, Jenny!'

Bodies turned and rushed madly by in case the brute breathed out and converted them into toast. All of a sudden I was at the front of the crowd and not the back – there was nothing between me and that Beast but a few dreadful feet of dark corridor; and rather than stop to say Hello I joined the stampede in the opposite direction.

We did not go quietly. Everybody was screaming. I was screaming myself and didn't even know it until I stopped doing it. We swarmed into the well-lit hall, everyone babbling at once.

'Now children, you are going to have to calm yourselves down,' said Mrs White, clapping her hands uselessly. Nobody could hear them in the din.

'It was green all over!'

'I saw its tongue, Mrs White.'

'I think it had spikes!'

'Oh be *quiet*, children, this is so silly. Mr Ford has gone to have a look.'

But would he come back alive, some of us were thinking.

He did. And something like silence fell at last, for Mr Ford is one of those rare people who refuse to shout. 'It's just as I thought,' he said. 'One of you thinks he sees something and the rest of you follow like silly panicking sheep. There is nothing in the corridor and there never was. Now get your coats on and leave the school in an orderly way.'

One or two relieved little faces began to smile again, but the rest of us knew better.

We didn't believe him.

Chapter 3

I CAN'T REMEMBER who first called it the Thursday Creature, but I think it was the one-and-only Ernest Kilbride.

Ernie is one of those people who can calculate the orbits of satellites in their supernormal brains. If you ask Ernie

where Kuala Lumpur is, first he'll tell you how to pronounce it right, then where it is, and whether it's day or night there at the time of asking. He tells you these things with a lovely modesty, and in a voice so soft you'd swear he was a spy passing secrets. I don't understand why he's so shy. If I had his brains I'd never be out of the limelight.

This Thing, this Thursday Creature, wasn't a dragon, Ernie said quietly at break time. He happened to be talking to his friend Stephen Bishop at the time, but since this was the queue for the tuck shop, millions of people were right there to contradict him.

'You weren't there, Kilbride,' Corinna pointed out. 'You're so wet you hardly ever come to Youth Club, so how can you know what it wasn't?'

Ernie blushed. 'I'm not saying I know anything about it.'

'Well, what are you saying?' Bishop asked, encouraging Ernie with a pleasant smile.

'It's just that there are many unexplained things in this life . . .'

'Talk English, Kilbride,' snapped Corinna.

'I am talking English. We don't have enough information yet, so we're

jumping to conclusions if we call it a dragon.'

'You'll jump out of your skin, Ernie I said, 'if it grabs you on your way to the loo. How can twenty people be wrong?'

Ernie's eyes were sad and brown and full of pity as he looked at me. 'People used to think that the Earth was flat, Jenny. If everybody in the whole world

was wrong about that, you could be wrong about this.'

Well, yes, I thought. That was one way to look at it if you wanted to. None of us did, though – we wanted dragons.

And all the while, I noticed, Bishop grinned as if he was enjoying all the fuss. I caught him looking at me once or twice, clearly sizing me up for a crushing defeat on Thursday night, and

I made a point of staring him down in case he got the idea that I was scared of him.

Which I was – a little. At least, I was scared of losing, and desperate to become Undisputed Quoits Champion of the Whole School. The thought of such glory took my breath away.

There was bad news on Thursday night because Bishop failed to turn up at Youth Club. I went to Mr Ford and tried to claim victory by Disqualification.

'Don't be ridiculous, Jenny,' said Mr Ford, 'we can play just as easily next week. Stephen was at a funeral today.'

'Not his own, I hope.'

'Jenny,' said Mr Ford, rather sharply.

He failed to understand the mental

torment I was in. Everybody went off to play something else – Quoits was now old hat – and I was left to practise on my own. Ernie offered to give me a game, but he was hopeless. We gave up after the quoit smashed into his nose and made it bleed.

'I'm not very good at that game,' he said, seriously contemplating his own blood.

'It's your first time, Ernie.'

'My last too, I should think. You should take a rubber ring and practise at home like Stephen.'

'You mean Bishop practises at *home*?' The sneak, I thought.

'Well, he told me he wants to beat you. Not because he doesn't like you, I don't mean that. I think he does, actually.'

'Does what?'

'Like you.'

'Has he been talking about me, Ernie?'

'Not really. He says you look nice.'

Well, fancy that, I thought, too amazed by far to say a word. Luckily Ernie was too busy inspecting his nose for further leaks to observe that my end of the conversation had dried up.

By the time Youth Club ended I felt more sorry for Ernie than for myself. He hadn't come along for the company or the quoits: he would have had a more thrilling time at home counting up to a million in prime numbers or something. No. He was here to see the Thursday Creature, and it kept him waiting right to the last minute.

I happened to be standing with my back to the cloakroom windows when I saw the grisly change come over Craig

Harvey's face. It turned a peculiar colour – jotter-page faded cream, I would call it – because the blood had said goodbye to his face and gone wherever blood goes when you're scared out of your skin.

'It's that Thing again!' he managed to croak.

Right behind me, I knew, was that It with a capital I. Ernie went as stiff as a

scarecrow and Melanie's voice hit the highest possible *doh* as if I could expect to feel hot breath on my neck at any moment.

I performed a pirouette, insanely preferring to face whatever was about to eat me, and saw that it was outside, oh blessed relief, beyond the glass and safely out of reach.

It was dark out there, but enough light got through the window to show us all that ugly head again and that mouth, all shiny, like the inside of a water-melon. The brute bashed its snout against the window frame in a fit of rage, then disappeared into the night.

'Well, Ernie?' I cried. 'Explain *that* away if you can!'

Ernie nodded, and eased out his breath as if he'd been hoarding it for quite some time. 'Well, yes. It's very impressive, isn't it?'

Then he began to make a note of coat-peg numbers like some batty professor who can't do without sums.

Chapter 4

BASICALLY, HUMAN BEINGS are capable of believing anything. I know this because I heard people talking about the Thursday Creature all through the following day.

Some people took the Common Sense approach. The Beast was an actual animal of some sort – an escaped orang-utan (Sandra Dale), even though the nearest zoo was fifty miles away; or a cow was loose in the neighbourhood (Melanie) and luckily this cow could see in the dark; or it was somebody dressed up (Ernie's theory).

Other people took the Freaked Out approach – we had a Thing From Outer Space on our hands, or else it was a

mutant from the sewers. The Big Chief
of this group of loonies was Jim Fender,
who is from outer space himself if you
ask me.

At home time I went along to the PE
store to borrow a quoit, and ran into
Stephen Bishop.

He said, 'Hi.'

I said, 'What are you doing?'

'Getting a quoit,' he said. 'I want to
get in some practice. Everybody says

you'll be a pushover.' And he smiled at me.

His smile was friendly and indeed rather nice, but the words made me bristle. 'Do they?'

'But I saw you beat Fender. You're fast. You won't be a pushover. Ernie says you're left-handed.'

'Ernie is a rotten cheap spy,' I said, 'and may his nose bleed till Christmas.'

Bishop laughed. It struck me that this was the first time I'd spoken to him except for that time when I called him a hacker. I took a yellow quoit, he took a green one, and we said Goodbye.

If you want to make people happy, bring home a rubber ring. That's all it takes. All of Saturday afternoon my Dad played quoits over the garden fence with our neighbour Mr Gilmore, who had played quoits on board ship while crossing the Equator way back in the days of Elvis Presley and black-and-white TV.

When Mr Gilmore had finished thrashing my poor father, he showed me how to throw a Big Dipper.

'Plenty of flick and a limp wrist, Jenny,' he said – but it wasn't easy.

And then on Sunday our poodle got in on the act. I was practising Big Dippers on my own when Marzipan pounced and ran away with it. That was why I sneaked into the PE store early on Monday morning with a chewed-up quoit, and buried it deep in the pile so that nobody would spot the teethmarks, I hope, for about a hundred years.

As I closed the door I heard another sound. It was quite muffled, but close by.

Our PE store is situated at the front of the hall, near the stage. There wasn't a soul in the whole place except myself, so I began to get that shiver-up-my-back feeling which tells me things aren't quite what they should be. It happened again – a muffled scrape followed by a dull thud.

Noises don't make themselves, this I knew for a scientific fact. My poor heart was jumping. If this was the Thursday Creature, what could I do all by myself alone? Then I heard footsteps at the far side of the stage.

Over there was a short stairway that disappeared below the level of the stage. Personally I'd no idea where it went, for I'd never been down there. Stephen Bishop came up those steps and went out a side door without spotting me.

What had he been up to? Curiosity is a very powerful thing and I'm not surprised that it kills cats. After hesitating for about two seconds I went down to see for myself.

At the bottom of the steps was a half-door held closed by a hefty bolt. You could tell just by looking at it that only special people like headmasters and caretakers were allowed in there.

All the same, I slid back the bolt and opened the door.

The smell of closed-in air came at me out of a pitch dark hole and I would not have taken one step forward if I hadn't noticed the switch on a beam just at my head. Fluorescent tubes flickered

crazily, then flooded the place with light.

The entire area under the stage was littered with heaps of desks and chairs from ages past. Many of the desks had little china ink-wells – I'm sure they were antiques. In a large wooden heart someone had carved the initials JK.

Well, I thought, if a school has an old attic then this is it! I saw broken easels and stately cupboards and a bundle of thin canes straight out of the days when naughty boys got six-of-the-best. At my feet, waiting to be tripped over, lurked an old globe with a hole in the middle of the Atlantic Ocean.

And where were they now, I wondered, all the teachers and pupils who had used this ancient educational furniture? Maybe poor old JK was pushing up the daisies. I was about to inspect a trunk full of clothes when a rumble of thunder burst about my ears.

Someone was walking on the stage just above my head. I knew I had to get out quickly or I would be trapped there all through Assembly. Luckily it was only Craig Harvey and another of Mr Ford's boys setting up the chairs – in our school it is always the boys who get to set up the chairs.

I managed to slip away without being seen.

Chapter 5

'HE IS, MELANIE,' I said. 'Stephen Bishop is the Thursday Creature. I am telling you this because I *know*.'

'I wouldn't be one bit surprised,' said Melanie. 'But what was he doing down there, under the stage?'

'It proves he's acting funny, and keep your voice down,' I added, as Corinna Bell walked by. She was on her way to the front of the class to deliver a talk on oil rigs. 'I bet he goes down there and changes into a monster costume every Thursday night and then creeps out to plunge the whole school into terror.'

Melanie gave a snigger, which is a kind of laugh involving the use of the nose. 'Did you find his monster costume when you were down there?'

'I didn't have time to look.'

'You don't think he might have been doing a job for the caretaker?'

'What job? The place is a graveyard for dead desks!'

'All right, I believe you.' Her eyes were wide with excitement. 'But Stephen Bishop wasn't at Youth Club on Thursday. You told me he was at a funeral.'

'Even if he was, he still might have done it. People don't get buried at night. Come down and see for yourself. We'll go at lunchtime when the hall's empty.'

'I can't, I've got recorder practice.'

'Tomorrow, then. And don't breathe a word of this, we'll keep it to ourselves.'

'As if I would, Jenny,' said Melanie – but I wasn't fooled for a minute by the loyal look in her eyes. She knows, and I know, that spreading secrets is the best kind of fun there is.

I walked home that afternoon. Mum was supposed to pick me up in the car but I can never rely on her. She has a small nursery business – plants, that is, not babies – and gets so tied up with petunias and things that she forgets about me, her most precious little flower of all.

I had reached the Co-op when the front wheel of a bike appeared on the footpath beside me. Stephen Bishop said Hello. My amazement must have showed in my face, for he did not dismount.

'How did your practice go?' he asked.

'Very well, thank you,' I said. This sounded ridiculous, I know it did.

'That's good.'

'Except the dog ran away with the quoit.'

This made him laugh and lose his balance. Now he was walking along beside me, wheeling his bike. What did he want?

'I broke a lampshade,' he said. 'It

took a long time to pick up all the glass.'

'I bet your Mum was pleased. Have you played quoits before?'

'No. Funny sort of game, isn't it?'

'It started on board ship,' I said. 'They used to play on deck while crossing the Equator.'

'Very interesting,' said Bishop. 'I suppose you can see why. If you kicked a football into touch it'd be in the ocean.'

'With the sharks,' I added, and we both laughed at the idea of soccer-playing sharks.

Am I really walking up Castle Street with the Thursday Creature, I found myself wondering.

Mum drew up with a *toot-toot* of the horn. Stephen Bishop waved goodbye to me, and to her, before riding off.

'See you on Thursday night,' he called.

Mum delivered her apologies. Her cuttings were wilting and she'd had to mist-spray. 'And who is your friend with the nice manners?' she inquired nosily.

'That was Stephen Bishop, Mother, and he is not my friend. That was the first time he's ever talked to me and I bet he was trying to spy out my tactics for the match.'

Mother gave a quiet little smile.

'Boys are not usually as complicated as that, Jenny. I think he probably just likes you, dear.'

I blushed a little, because I thought she was probably right.

During Tuesday lunchtime I sneaked under the stage with Melanie and she didn't like it down there because it was spooky and crawling with spiders, she said – as if we were in some dark dungeon in Transylvania. I told her to

wise up and start looking.

First we turned out the contents of the trunk and found enough stuff in there to dress the whole school as Wise Men and shepherds. And then, so help me, I saw It grinning up at me from a shadowy corner and my heart gave an awful jolt, for that Beast was anything but pretty to look at.

Really, it was a kind of painted horse – the kind they have in pantomimes.

Its mouth, scarlet on the inside, gaped
open, and was full of outsized, horsey
teeth. The demented look in its wild,
white eyes gave me the shivers, but
Melanie is one of those people who sees
a horse of any description, and just
melts.

'Oh look, he's so cute,' she said in a
voice of sugar.

When she picked up the head, the back
legs remained on the ground. Its cloth
body was greenish yellow with darker
spots. Melanie slipped on the head
and I heard her have a muffled fit of
the giggles.

'If you could see yourself from out
here, Melanie, you wouldn't be
laughing.'

'And you think it's Stephen Bishop,
said the horse.

'Maybe.'

'You were dead sure yesterday it was him.'

'Well I've been talking to him since that. Actually, he walked home with me yesterday.'

Off came the horse's head like a flash. 'You're kidding! He walked home with you?'

'Part of the way, yes.'

'You and who else?'

'Nobody else.'

'Well you didn't tell me that! I think he must like you, Jenny.'

'Oh for goodness' sake, Melanie,' I retorted, 'he wanted to talk about quoits. And on Thursday night we're going to watch him like a hawk. If he *is* the Thursday Creature, we're going to nail him for sure.'

Chapter 6

YOU MIGHT EASILY imagine that all the wild stories about the Thursday Creature would keep people away from Youth Club. Let's face it, if you've got a goat like Fender trying to convince the whole world that a werewolf will rip open throats and slurp up the warm blood, it's not exactly wonderful publicity.

Why, then, was the place packed on Thursday evening?

I guess most people suspected by now that the creature was a clever trick. If you really believe in werewolves you don't go near places where you might bump into one. All the same, I noticed that nobody went to

the toilets alone – they travelled in
gangs, just in case. Poor Mrs White
became hoarse trying to control the
simmering excitement.

I had trouble trying to control
myself when Mr Ford announced the
final of the Quoits Championship.
Stephen Bishop came up to me and said
Good Luck, which I suppose was nice of
him. I wished him Good Luck in
return, but didn't mean a word of it. I

wanted all the luck that was going.

Mr Ford cleared away the mob from the centre of the Hall and put up the cord. And now, with spectators lining both sides of the playing area, our Hall had become a Theatre. Jennifer Graham, I told myself, here is your Centre Court. I felt like I'd swallowed an electric mixer and it was churning up my tea.

We played the first point. My supporters chanted my name so loudly that it was embarrassing, frankly, and didn't help me a bit. I played like a robot with ten tin thumbs for a point or two.

'Five—three to Bishop,' called Mr Ford.

The game was half over already! I produced my first Big Dipper on the next point – plenty of flick, loose wrist

– and the quoit barely made it over the cord. It hit the floor with a lovely thud as Bishop dived to meet it.

The Big Dipper.

Five–all. Then it was six–all. Across the cord I saw his eyes and his tight mouth and the sweat was tripping him. Did *I* look like that? People were shouting my name and I felt like a million dollars. Basically, I think I was meant to be a star.

I was winning seven–six when he started to Wobble the Quoit. Instead of coming into my hand smoothly, it spun like a tossed coin in the air, and when I tried to catch the thing it behaved as if it was alive and jumped six feet into the audience.

Corinna picked up it. 'Try catching it this time,' she said.

'Why don't you die off!' I snapped back.

'Never mind, Jenny, *concentrate!*' Sandra shrieked at me.

Sandra Dale isn't even in my class,

we are practically strangers. This made me see how I was fighting for the honour of all girls everywhere. Even Corinna Bell!

I sent back a vicious twister-dipper and he had no chance.

'Nine–eight to Bishop,' called Mr Ford, and suddenly it was match-point already! Was I doomed? My hands shook as I flung the quoit as if I never wanted to see it again.

Stephen Bishop snapped back a throw, but too quickly. I joyfully watched it pass *under* the cord – or so I thought. But instead of saying nine–all, Mr Ford announced, 'Bishop wins the game ten–eight.'

I couldn't speak. I swallowed and I swallowed. 'But it went under the cord,' I said. 'It was a foul throw.'

'Jenny – you lost,' said Mr Ford.

I was shattered and ready to weep
rivers of tears. My Dad says that
people who argue with referees are
ruining sport but I didn't want to
argue, I just wanted to shoot the
referee dead and instead I had to grin
and bear it when Bishop stepped
forward to shake my hand.

'You played great,' he said.

And you are gloating inside with secret glee, I thought. 'Not great enough.'

'It could have gone either way, really.'

'But it didn't.'

I parked myself on a bench, wondering why on earth people go on playing sport when there's only one winner to scoop up all the happiness.

'Oh Jenny, you were marvellous,' said Melanie, plonking herself down beside me.

'Well I don't feel it. His last throw went *under* the cord – did you see?'

'I don't think it did. Really, Jenny, nobody thinks it did. Anyway, it's not the end of the world.'

Probably not. It was the end of my quoit-playing days for ever, though. I happened to glance up at the stage, and saw that the back curtain had been pulled – the one that conceals the stairway to the room below. Melanie saw it too, and stared at me with eyes as round as quoits.

The Thursday Creature was getting ready.

Chapter 7

MELANIE AND I crouched breathlessly at the bottom of the stairs like a couple of cowards. The bolt had been drawn back, so there was definitely somebody in there.

'You go in first, Jenny.'

'What'll I say, Melanie! I can't just burst in and say "Hands up, you Beast", can I?'

There we were, dithering together, when all of a sudden the door opened inwards and we were staring straight at Stephen Bishop.

'It *was* you!' I burst out.

'Me what?'

'You're that Thursday thing, that . . . horse!'

He told us to keep our voices down, then beckoned with a finger for us to follow him under the stage, which we did. Perched up on a redundant vaulting-horse like an owl upon a branch, was Ernie the Wise in shining specs.

Surely not Ernie, I thought!

'It wasn't me, Jenny,' Stephen Bishop said, looking right at me, and I stared right back, believing him.

Maybe it was the quiet way he suddenly made my name sound like one of the lovely words of the English language. 'If you look you'll see that the horse is already gone.'

It was – but only the head bit. The back legs lay in a heap.

'We know who it is, though,' said Ernie, sliding off his perch, 'and we'd better go. We probably haven't got much time.'

Well for heaven's sake who is it, I wanted to know, but Ernie was in too much of a hurry to listen to questions as he fixed a chain lock through the bolt on the door. 'Off my bike,' he said, 'in case it slips by us.' This forward planning made me realise how dangerous Ernie would be to the police if he ever turned crooked.

'Through the canteen!' he shouted in a whisper. 'That's the way it comes and goes. Come on.'

'Okay, Ernie,' said Melanie, 'who is it? Tell us.'

'You'll be amazed when you see.'

Mr Ford? Or Mrs White, I wildly thought. As we left the gloomy canteen Ernie tied the doors together by the handles with a piece of thin rope he just happened to have in his pocket, and I saw that the poor creature had finally met its match. It had no chance.

We held a short meeting to discuss tactics. 'It's going to hide in the dark under the stairs that lead up to the staffroom,' Ernie said. 'Jenny – you and Melanie walk by as if you're talking about something. As soon as she makes her move, I'll hit the lights.'

She, I thought. The Thursday Creature was a girl?

I'll say this for her – she was a pretty good actress. Even though I knew she was a fake I still jumped like a flea when that head loomed up in front of me. As soon as the lights came on, however, the creature seemed to curl up with fear, just like Count Dracula when the sun peeps over the hill. And in two shakes of a lamb's tail, as my Dad would say, the terrifying had become the ridiculous. Here was a horse's head wearing blue jeans below. It panicked and made a bolt for the canteen.

There was no way through, of course. Back it came. We blocked the dark corridor, so it veered towards the well-lit cloakrooms, where several groups of potato-crisp eaters could hardly believe their luck.

'Hey! What was that?'

'The dragon!'

'Get it!'

Strange whooping noises echoed down the corridor like the Apaches after John Wayne. For the next few minutes, while the chase lasted, our school was a mad-house. The creature managed to hide in a nook between the medical room and the library, but Fender the Ferret soon flushed it out again, and they greeted it like an old frien

'Here, horsey-horsey – sugar lumps.'

'Oh, it's shy.'

In the end, giving up the race, the exhausted beast lurched into the Hall and turned to face its tormentors.

'Take off your head at once! Take it off. Take off that head, I say!' shrieked Mrs White, impersonating a parrot.

The head came off and it was knock-me-down-with-a-feather time. Sandra Dale was the Thursday Creature.

Her face was the colour of a boiled lobster's claw, and sweaty with the effort of trying to escape from the mob. The poor thing slumped to the floor and sobbed her heart out. Melanie sniffed in sympathy because it's always awful to see somebody so miserable.

Mr Ford took Sandra by the elbow and gently raised her up. 'Why have you been doing this, Sandra?'

There was a hysterical wail. 'I don't know, Mr Ford, it was only a joke. I just saw it one day and I wanted to wear it and . . . and . . . and I did wear it but I thought people would only *laugh* and then . . . I wanted to stop but something *made* me do it!'

There are many teachers who would have stuck her in front of a firing squad, but he was wonderful. 'The question is, have you learned anything from this nonsense, Sandra?'

'I have, yes I have.'

'Put it back where it came from, then, and if you've learned your lesson we'll say no more about it. What do you think, Mrs White?'

Mrs White looked as though she wanted Sandra's head on a silver plate, but her lips remained as tightly closed as a miser's purse. Then she clapped her hands busily. 'Come along, children, please. Get your coats and hurry on home. I think we've had quite enough excitement for one night.'

The Thursday excitement wasn't quite over yet, though – not for me. I caught Stephen Bishop's eye above a row of coat pegs.

'Don't think you'll be so lucky the next time,' I told him, just in case he was feeling too pleased with himself.

He gave me a lovely friendly smile as he fiddled with the indoor shoes strung round his neck.

'I wonder are you going up the road, Jenny?' he asked me.

I made him wait a little while for my answer. But I knew the road he meant – and yes, I was going that way.